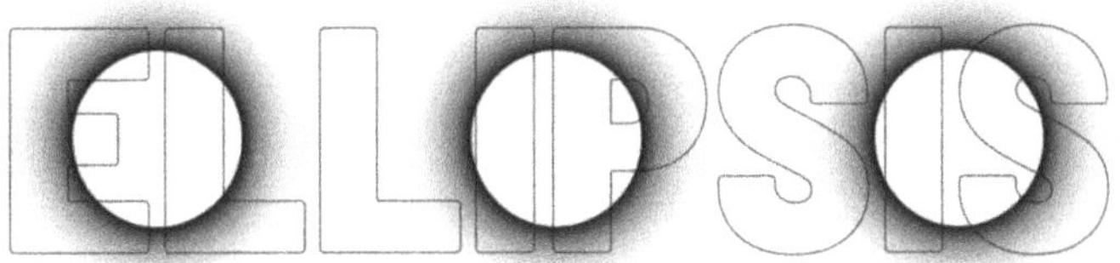

Short Stories by

C.A. Lynne

SCARMORA PRESS

A Message from C.A. Lynne

Science fiction and fantasy stories captivated me as a child, sparking my imagination and creativity. I soon started crafting my own tales, as each new story was an opportunity to explore uncharted territory and experience a life far different from my own. Though fictional, their struggles always felt familiar. I found joy in giving voice to their stories as unknown realms become vivid and characters come alive through my writing.

Now as an author, that excitement remains. I still lose myself in storytelling, transported to new places with each new work. Whether crafting epics or quieter stories, my goal is to honour the narratives inspired by my imagination. There are always more worlds to build and characters to discover, and I strive to vividly bring their stories to life on the page.

Table of Contents

Storm Season

Rule 1: Don't look.

Rule 2: Don't engage.

Rule 3: Use the light.

Rule 4: Use cinnamon.

Rule 5 ...

Addie tapped her foot restlessly while staring out the kitchen window at the trees blowing in the wind. The winds had been picking up the last few days and she realized she was not prepared for this year's storm season. The clinking of metal and banging on the walls behind her told her there was quite a bit she was supposed to have done before this. The skies had already turned sepia, clouds rolled in from the west. It was coming earlier and earlier each year; she should have been preparing like everyone else.

"All set ma'am," the voice said behind her after the clanking and banging had ceased. "You know you were really cutting it close this year. You had a few windows that needed resealing. And the front door."

Addie turned to the man and saw the sweat beading down his temples. She gave him a polite smile.

"Yes, thank you. I just—my husband died earlier this year, he usually handles this, so I didn't think," she said, drifting off. The man gave her a look of pity.

"I'm sorry to hear. Don't you have anyone to spend the season with?" he asked.

"No, they're too far away, and I won't trouble them. I'll be fine. I've got the dog," she said, eyeing the lazy mutt on the living room rug.

"Well, if that's all then. You're all set. You be careful now. It'll strike any day."

And with that, the repair man was off, leaving Addie to the silence of her home, save for the rustling of the trees and whirring of the wind. Soon the whistling of her teapot rang out and she settled herself down in the living room with her mutt, wondering just how long she had until the storm hit. It'd be the first in a very long time that she spent alone, she realized. She had only been out of her parents' house for three years when she met Sam, and even though they hadn't officially moved in together until the summer after that, she had spent the storm with him. If you could, you were best off spending it in company. Loners were most vulnerable. When she was twenty, she had laughed at that notion of course, and rode out the storm fearlessly. Now though, after seeing nearly twenty more, she understood the reason behind that saying, and it made her shiver even as she sipped her hot tea.

But she did have the dog. Biscuit may be lazy, but he was a good and faithful boy, and always alert during the storm. He had never let anything slip past them all these years. She knew that without Sam here this year, she could count on Biscuit to be her second set of eyes. As if hearing her thoughts, he raised his head at her and inched closer to sleep on her feet, calming her as she stared out the living room window at the street where little children played, getting their last runs in before the first rain drops ushered them in behind locked doors.

The next morning, the clouds were still full, the pavement still dry and ready. It was holding out as long as possible, which could only mean it would be a long and painful storm once it hit. Addie wondered if she had time for one more grocery trip; she would hate to run out of bread or water while waiting it out. She heaved a sigh, gritting her teeth against the decision, knowing what it could mean if she were caught in the storm, but decided to make the run just down the street to the mart, taking Biscuit with her.

Michael's shop was still open; his apartment lay right above the little mart, so he could keep it running right up until the first raindrops. Pulling right up to the front parking spot, she raced in with Biscuit in tow and nodded to Michael at the counter.

"Addie, I thought you'd be locked in by now. It's comin'!" Michael said, counting the register. Jimmy, another old-timer like Michael, finished his purchase and nodded at Addie before ducking out of the store. "We're all closin' up this afternoon."

"I know, I just was getting worried I didn't have enough," she said. Michael nodded and continued his closing duties as Addie rushed around, grabbing a case of water and other foods on top. Biscuit trailed behind her silently, sniffing for treats down the aisles until Addie found them and let him walk them up to the counter.

"The news says it's gonna be a long one," he said, nodding at the TV behind him.

"...that all emergency services will cease today at three," she heard one of the anchors say.

"Some counties have already closed off," the co-anchor chimed in. "We have not gotten word of the first rainfall, but some areas are looking at four days..."

Addie turned away from the screen and looked out the window where the wind was stirring up litter. She had been through longer storms, of course, but now four days seemed a lot to get through on her own.

"You best get back, and lock up now," Michael said as he rang her up.

"Thank you, Michael," Addie said, and he tossed Biscuit a treat from his stash.

She drove home as fast as she could, feeling the eeriness falling deeper over the town now. The sepia turned to a dark haze, and the wind dropped to a stillness that happened just before everything came crashing down. She could feel goosebumps from her head down through her whole body, but she slowed her breathing and tried to ease herself as she pulled into her driveway, the sound of the pebbles breaking the quiet around her. She looked at Biscuit, who seemed to know with his big brown eyes what they needed to do.

She opened the door quickly and rushed to the other side of the car, opening the door for Biscuit, who rushed up to the back door and waited for her as she grabbed her groceries and walked briskly up the porch steps. In the corner of her eye, she caught the rush of the trees and something else, a shadow maybe, when she looked up from setting the groceries down. She didn't have time to wonder what it was. She could see raindrops. She fumbled for her housekey as Biscuit stood behind her and started growling. It sent a chill up her spine as she opened the door and tossed the grocery bags into the kitchen, not worrying about the food tumbling out of the bags onto the floor.

"Let's go Biscuit," she called, rushing inside over the rolling food. But she turned to close the door behind him, and he wasn't there following. "Biscuit!"

She took a cautious step out onto the back porch, trying to see where he'd gone off to. He was behind her not a minute before. She heard a bark in the distance and without thought, ran to the edge of the porch to see him chasing something off in the distance. His haunches were raised, and his tail was down; he was defending the property as the rain started coming down. The storm was here, and she needed to get him inside.

"Biscuit! Come on, boy, let's go!" she yelled. He backed away from whatever he was fighting off, and then turned away, content that he was successful, and came racing back to her. But in the corner of Addie's eye, she saw another shadow and she ran back to where she had left the front door open. No, she thought shaking her head. No, no, no. Biscuit quickly ran in after it and she knew it couldn't have been her imagination. But behind her, she could see more shadows forming and she had to take a chance. She couldn't stay outside anymore. The wind was already swirling around her and the sky was deepening. Rushing inside against the rising shadows, she pushed her body into the door, leaning against it and falling to the ground with heavy, nervous breaths.

She closed her eyes. She wanted to cry. She reached up, remembering to lock the door. Remembering her breathing, she drew in a deep breath through her nose and out her mouth. She continued her breaths, calming herself down, listening to the roaring winds pick up outside. In front of her, she could hear Biscuit breathing too, panting rather, in the living room. And then a growl had her leaping from the tiled floor and she was on her feet with her back to the door. It was dark inside her home, she hadn't left any lights on. It was hardly midday, though, she didn't think it was going to get dark this soon. But once the storm hit, it looked either dusk or night the entire length of it.

She could just barely see Biscuit standing in the doorway between the dining room and the living room as she leaned out of the kitchen, stepping over food and not even bothering to deal with it until she knew for sure what was, or wasn't, inside her house. Biscuit stood frozen with a low growl, but the source of his aggression she could not see. As she stepped through the dining room, creaking along the old wood floors, she thought she heard a soft giggle that froze the breath in her throat and her feet in their place. She dared not move an inch closer to where Biscuit eyed the possible intruder. She hoped, prayed, wished; she did all she could to make it all go away. She closed her eyes tight again.

"I won't hurt you." Addie cringed and let out a shriek. The dog barked and growled loudly but Addie stayed frozen beside the dining table. How could this happen? Sam had never let them get in, and in her first storm without him, she had failed.

"Please," the voice called out again. A woman's voice. Addie kept her eyes closed, determined to ignore it. She tried to remember the rules, the protocol for if one should ever get inside. Rule 1. Don't look at them. Rule 2. Don't engage with them. Rule 3. Rule 3. What was Rule 3? Why couldn't she remember the rest of the rules?

Biscuit continued to growl, but the growl grew closer, which meant she was moving. It was moving, Addie reminded herself. They were not people. They pretended to get to us, she thought. She had heard several years back of one pretending to be a family's lost child, standing out in the rain, banging on the door for hours until the mother couldn't take it anymore. The family tried to keep her from it but in the end, she went out and they locked the door behind her, never to see her again. That was the next town over. Nothing like that ever happened here. This town had never had an incident. Until now, she thought.

But she was determined. Rule 1. Don't look at them. Rule 2. Don't engage with them. Rule 3. Stay in the light. Yes, she needed light, as much light as possible. The switch was behind her; she reached around and fumbled along the wall, but there it was. The dining room flooded with illumination from the overhead chandelier, and she was able to open her eyes, knowing it wouldn't be in the room anymore. If the power went out, she would have to figure things out. She did have the generator, but the hookup was in the basement, and she wasn't sure what light was connected to it. It was minimal, meant for the fridge and a few other things. She hoped it would be a last resort.

Rule 4. Repel with cinnamon. Cinnamon! She remembered. Of course, she thought, she always had cinnamon in the house. Everyone did now. Cautiously turning around, she went back to the kitchen, carefully stepping into the lighted area to find the switch for the kitchen. In her spice cupboard, she found the large container of cinnamon, still very full. She hardly baked anymore since Sam had passed. She opened the lid and smelled it, nearly choking on it as it went up her nose. It would be worse on them, she thought. Now to remember how it worked. It had been years since she learned the rules, and she never thought she would ever have to use them. Especially Rule 5. If all else fails, don't let them take you. There was a reason the storms were getting worse every year.

As she headed through the house turning on all the lights, she glimpsed the shadow swirling, escaping to each dark corner left until it had nowhere else to go. Addie powdered the cinnamon across her rugs and sensed the unease in the atmosphere, the discomfort from her restless intruder, and she started to feel somewhat relaxed. She had forced it into a cage of sorts, backed into a corner with nothing to feast on. Addie felt a wave of strength come over her for a moment and almost had an idea of dumping the cinnamon right on top of the creepy little pest and hunting it down, but she thought better of it, knowing the power could go out at any moment, and the creature would have its strength back. How effective the cinnamon was, she couldn't be sure. For now, Addie was content keeping it at bay until she could devise some other strategy, for she would need something else before the storm was through.

In her pajamas with a comfy blanket and book, her hot tea and the cinnamon beside her, Addie tried to relax with Biscuit sitting on watch. She knew it would be hard to sleep even with all the lights on, even with a ring of cinnamon around them, even with all the safeties and precautions. So she took to reading. The storm rumbled outside, thundering and clawing at the sky, rain pattering at the roof and windows. She had long since shuttered everything, not wanting any notion of the shadows that lingered. She wondered if they would come for the one stuck inside, if they even knew it was here, if they even had that kind of connection.

"Please," the voice called, and she stiffened. "Please help me."

It was a rather soft voice for such a thing. The shadows that lurked in the storm. But it only took the form that appealed to her senses, she thought. She ignored it, reading her book and trying not to watch it in the corner of her eye as the lights flickered down the stairs, retreating from a shadow made by the tall chair on the opposite side of the room.

Rule 1. Don't look at them. She kept her eyes on the book even though in her peripheral now, the shadow rose above the chair, standing in the figure of a girl. She realized she was still reading the same line, trying to concentrate on the chapter in front of her but getting distracted by the evil lurking in her living room. She clenched her jaw, determined to follow the rules and not bend to its will.

"Please, you must protect me from them."

Addie told herself it wasn't real. It was just some ruse. There wasn't anyone she needed protection from. She came with the storm. *It*, she reminded herself. They weren't people. She repeated it; they were not people. Shadows lurking in the storm.

Rule 2. Don't engage with them. She sipped her tea, and put it down, taking the cinnamon and tapping it out in the direction of the shadow. The shadow gasped and shrank back into the darkness of the chair. But after a while, the lights flickered with the rumbling of the thunder and the shadow was out in full again. Addie knew it was only a matter of time before she lost power. And she couldn't stay awake for a week straight either way. She would have to figure out a way to get rid of the shadow. There were no other rules besides Rule 5. Of course, the rule was open to interpretation, everyone she had seen on the news at the close of each season had interpreted it the same way. She would not let it come to that.

"Please help me." It was getting rather annoying now, this call for help.

Like Addie would fall for it. Sam might have, though this wouldn't have happened with him here in the first place. He was the sympathetic one of the two. Addie recalled he was the one who brought Biscuit home one day seven years ago, saved from a box on the side of the road with his other siblings. They gave away the other pups to families in town; they all grew up to be such good watch dogs Addie wondered why anyone would ever just give them up. Biscuit growled again at the shadow now as it lingered in the faint figure of a girl in the corner by the chair. Addie rubbed his head and wondered why they weren't affected the same way by looking directly at them as humans were. Without an answer, she was just grateful she had a companion to watch it for her.

Addie woke with a start to Biscuit's barking and she realized she had drifted off to sleep sometime in the night while reading. He was standing with the front paws outside the circle of cinnamon, haunches raised as he aimed his aggression toward the darkened corner of the staircase. Some of the lights were out, but not all, so the power was still on. It must have been doing something, trying to take out the lights, she thought, and Biscuit caught it. She took a cautious peek out the window to see it was daytime with the wind still beating away at the trees, blowing debris down the street and sending sheets of rain across the earth. She could just barely make out the whirls of shadows tearing their way through the rain before shielding her eyes and shutting the blinds. There were so many, she thought. More than she remembered last year. She knew the toll was growing each year, but she thought with all the raised precautions it would somehow get better. But then Addie eyed the dark corner of her own home and her stomach churned.

"Will you help me now?" the shadow said almost with desperation. Addie was surprised it could mimic that kind of emotion. They were learning. It was rather annoying, the thing, with its stupid plea. But she was determined to follow the rules. She quickly grabbed the cinnamon and scattered more of it around as she checked on the lights. Her house was beginning to smell like cinnamon already. But she didn't mind. It's not like she had a choice, really. Cinnamon or die, she thought. But Biscuit was starting to stir it up, she could feel it tickling her nose now, there was so much on the rugs. He still stood guard watching the corner of the stairs as Addie readjusted the light bulbs and clicked the lamps on again. She powdered the rest of the first floor as she walked to the kitchen to start boiling water for tea. The lights continued flickering as the shadow tried to come out, but the growling and cinnamon seemed to keep it at bay.

With a fresh cup of tea in one hand, and the cinnamon in the other, Addie returned to her spot on the sofa and opened her book. It was a silly romance novel, one set in a remote beach town. She wished she was there; they had planned to take a vacation this year after the season ended, get away from their quaint middle-class suburb. It had been years since she traveled by herself though, and if she couldn't share the experience with Sam, what was the point? The books were enough to satisfy her wanderlust, she told herself. And at least enough to pull her mind away from the present situation.

After a while, Biscuit settled in beside her on the floor and seemed to ease his guard as the shadow slinked further into the corner. With another chapter and cup of tea down, Addie checked the time; it was almost noon. She looked down at Biscuit and wondered if it was safe to leave him while she used the bathroom. She settled on leaving the door open and listening for danger. She glanced around and noticed every corner was alight and visible. No places for the shadow to creep in where she was vulnerable, she thought with relief.

Addie then settled on lunch, rummaging through two weeks of frozen meals and finally picking the meatloaf and mashed potatoes, tossing it in the microwave before peeking into the living room. Everything looked fine, Biscuit was even still sleeping. Comfortably, too, she thought, seeing small twitches of dreaming. The shadow still lingered in the corner, but it seemed inactive. Could it be the exposure to the cinnamon, or the light? Or was it doing this on purpose? Addie shook away the fears.

But even after dinner and several chapters of her book, the shadow remained quiet in the corner. Addie could feel herself drifting off as it got later, and she knew she would have to sleep somehow. She scanned her rooms and found the bathroom was indeed the only place clear of shadows or crevices. So she pulled her king comforter off the bed and folded it into the tub with her pillow, Biscuit's bed on the floor across from her. She set up her book, lantern, and cinnamon to be in easy reach on the edge of the tub. It wasn't the most uncomfortable place, though she couldn't stretch out her legs. It would have to do for a couple more nights if she was going to have any peace of mind going to sleep.

Just as she nestled in and closed her eyes, she heard a wail from outside the bathroom that startled her stiff. It wasn't loud, just enough to echo in the tub. Biscuit perked up at the sound. Addie waited, listening for anything after that. Sure enough, the thing began whimpering. Crying, it was crying, she thought. She clenched her eyes shut and tried to think of sleeping. As the whimpering steadied, Addie was able to drift off, but periodically the thing would let out a high-pitched whine and she had to start over and settle her mind. Biscuit didn't seem to have trouble tuning out her cries. Its cries, she said to herself. It, it, it, she repeated. She thought about sleep and the world faded away from her, though the faint whines lingered in her ears.

Eventually, Addie found herself staring out of focus at the shower head, unable to sleep anymore. She leaned over the tub to see if she could read the alarm clock on her nightstand. It felt like a full night was gone, but she knew for sure she didn't get a full night's sleep. Maybe an hour or two at a time, but her worries and those cries kept her from reaching any level of rest. As she climbed out of the tub, she realized that it was more uncomfortable than it let on; her joints ached as she stood and stretched. Splashing her face with water, she rubbed her eyes awake and looked at herself in the mirror. She certainly looked as tired as she felt, but she was past sleeping now.

Addie decided against the risk of a shower, instead getting dressed and brushing her hair to some semblance of presentable so she could feel more prepared to start the day. It was only six, earlier than she was used to. Sam was the early riser, getting up before the sun; she liked sleeping in until the sun warmed her face. She peeked out the shuttered window in the bedroom and saw the dark of the storm was still hovering overhead. She closed it quickly with unease, and with that, she went downstairs for breakfast.

"You left me all alone," the voice broke the air as the stairs creaked under Addie's feet. Addie sighed and paused at the bottom step, not quite prepared to face that thing again. Ignoring it, she made her way to the kitchen, turning on the stove for tea and tossing bread in the toaster. She had her breakfast in the dining room as her radio scanned channels looking for updates on the storm, Biscuit enjoying his own breakfast by the table.

"—Reeling through hard over some regions," she heard and stopped the radio on that channel. "But I'm getting reports that the storm is directly over the county now, making its way toward the river tonight."

"Well, buddy, looks like it's almost over," she said out loud to Biscuit, turning the radio down. He could certainly understand most of what she said, or at least he acted like he did. The radio DJ went on about the storm, giving his personal view on how it wasn't as bad as the storm of '84. Addie laughed; even she didn't remember specific storm seasons, especially one from almost twenty years ago. The lights flickered overhead and she stood up alert.

"They're coming, you have to help me," the voice called, though Addie couldn't see where the shadow had crept. Biscuit's ears perked up, but he wasn't growling.

"Alright, Biscuit, let's clean up breakfast, and we'll watch a movie today," she said aloud, more for herself than the dog. Picking up her plate, she turned toward the kitchen but stopped short at the sight of a fleeting shadow. Ahead of her in the kitchen, the dark kitchen, she saw eyes. They were sad eyes, glowing with the dining room light that seeped in. Now Biscuit yelped and Addie nearly dropped her plate but clutched it hard as she averted her eyes.

Rule 1. Don't look at them. No, she thought. They had locked eyes, and she couldn't get that image out of her mind. Those sad eyes. Not real, she told herself. How could she have turned off the kitchen light? She stepped gingerly into the kitchen and flipped the switch, but the light didn't come on. She switched it again and again, hoping it would work. But again and again, nothing happened. She needed the kitchen. She set her plate down and looked at Biscuit, who was steady by her side. She would have to make it work. So they headed upstairs to find more light. She would have to sacrifice a room, she realized. Taking two lamps out of her office and shutting the door, she brought them down just outside the kitchen. She used the lantern to make a path into the kitchen and slowly plugged in both lamps. It made just enough light to go between the stove and fridge. There was a lot of shadow, but it would have to do. She outlined the lighted area with cinnamon, hoping to seal off the darkness. As the cinnamon dust settled, she heard giggles leave the room and echo out into the living room. It made her shiver.

Addie grabbed a handful of movies from the cupboard by the television and tried to settle into the couch. She saw the eyes again in her mind but shook her head and turned to the movie as the beginning credits rolled. She couldn't let herself think about it. But she broke a rule. What would happen now? So far, nothing. It still wasn't coming after her, so looking at it must not have been fatal, but she still felt her gut drop at the feeling of it watching her now with those eyes. She was still in danger, no matter how many barriers she made, no matter how well she followed the rules.

"Do you want to know what they are?" the voice asked and Addie flinched. It was now trying to make conversation? Addie turned up the volume on the television. "You can't let them get in, they're coming."

Addie ignored the pleas, turning the volume up more, forcing herself to focus on the movie. Once it got to the action sequences, it was almost too loud for Addie, but she didn't care. She needed the noise. Eventually, Biscuit was asleep again, and the house was calm. When the movie ended, she quickly jumped up to grab another one. She hummed to herself to make noise while she switched discs and continued to play it loudly. The shadow attempted her pleas and cries still, but Addie had found her solution, she realized. She could play all her movies on a loop for the next two or three days. She wouldn't be able to read with that much noise, but at least it would cover the incessant whining of that *thing*.

The next movie came to an end, but Addie left it on through the credits with the music playing as she went to the bathroom and got lunch ready, heating up another frozen meal in the microwave. She was careful not to step out of her cinnamon outline and kept her lantern by her side. Addie yawned as the microwave beeped and then remembered she would still have to try to sleep at some point. But the idea of sleeping brought back the image of that shadow looking at her. Would she be able to sleep with those eyes creeping back into her mind? If the radio was saying it was almost over anyway, did she need that much sleep? Maybe a few naps would be enough to break up the long hours she was enduring. She laughed at herself. She was now trying to ration her sleep? Biscuit tilted his head at her and she tossed him a treat.

Four movies, two crosswords, and one dinner later, Addie was yawning as often as she was blinking. She shook her head. She was a fool to think she could stay up as long as possible. And aside from a handful of attempts to speak, the shadow had grown quiet again. One quick whistle to Biscuit and they were headed upstairs to the bathroom and Addie's makeshift bed. It was oddly quiet now without the television; every movement felt thunderous as it broke the newfound silence. Addie nestled into the tub, barely able to keep her eyes open now. Biscuit spun around three times and curled up in his bed, looking pretty content. He had gotten sleep throughout the day. And if he was comfortable enough to rest, then she shouldn't be so worried. She sunk into the pillow and found sleep before she could think about it.

"No!" a shriek shook Addie out of sleep. She looked around at the bathroom. It was still brightly lit, but next to her, Biscuit was gone. "No! Don't let them in!"

The cries, growls, banging sounds. She couldn't make out what was going on. Her heart raced as she jumped up from the tub and ran out of the room toward the stairs.

"Biscuit!" she called, unsure where the growling was coming from. On the landing of the stairs, she saw half the lights out in the living room below. Something was banging on the walls outside, getting louder and closer like it was circling the house. And then she heard a yelp in the dining room, and she rushed over, careful to stay in the lighted areas of the living room. There she could see Biscuit cornered, barking at something in the kitchen. He hovered in the light, not able to move from the room. Outside, the banging followed her to the dining room windows. She pointed her lantern at the dark space between her and the dog, whistling for him to come back. He backed himself toward Addie, still growling at the shadow in the kitchen.

"Please don't hurt me," she heard it call. Addie could see its glowing eyes in her peripheral and she forced herself not to look up as Biscuit met her. They eased their way back up to the bathroom to gather the supplies and convened back in the living room, adjusting the bulbs until some came back on and illuminated most of the room.

The wind and banging outside had calmed down. Addie looked at the clock over the television; she had gotten two hours of sleep. She took a deep breath and resigned herself to the unfortunate truth of her situation. She was not safe. She inserted another movie and let it start playing while she gathered enough light to reach the kitchen and start the coffeemaker. The shadow cowered from her light as she fumbled through the kitchen for the coffee.

"I'm going to need help if I'm going to stay awake through the rest of this storm," she said aloud to herself. "I don't think I have any creamer left though."

She checked the fridge and saw she was out of creamer, but she shrugged and hummed to herself as a distraction from the thing she shared the room with. Once the coffee was brewed, she took the whole pot and a mug back to the living room with her.

"We'll just have to drink it black, Biscuit," she said as she settled on the couch and opened another crossword while the movie played in the background.

"You have to help me," she heard as the lights flickered from the shadow's movement. Back in the corner by the stairs, she saw.

"A term of endearment, seven letters," Addie spoke aloud, ignoring the voice. "Ah, 'darling.' Sam used to call me his darling, remember?" Biscuit nudged her hand with his nose at Sam's name. She knew he remembered. She gave him a pat and sipped her coffee, glancing at the movie in between crossword clues.

She tried to force herself into a routine. Bathroom break during the movie credits, a snack or meal with each fresh pot of coffee, humming or singing aloud while she changed discs. She remained in her small bubble of light as much as she could, only venturing out when necessary. The clock on the wall ticked away, but it was the pile of discs that showed her how time was passing. By the third movie, she had steady caffeine jitters but was still yawning and her body ached for the rest it needed. She stretched and changed positions, but it lingered in her bones.

On one side, her gentle companion slept but stirred frequently, and on the other, her unintended guest still sighed and cried softly. She continued asking for help, asking for protection from *them*. But she was one of *them*.

"It," she corrected herself out loud. Addie was certain the thing was trying to trick her. But she couldn't help but wonder why it chose this way to get to her. Did she really think she could convince Addie she was innocent?

By midday, the wind was still whirring outside, and rain batted on the roof without relenting. Addie peeked out the window while her food cooked, but it was still grey and stormy as yesterday and the day before. How long had it been now? She couldn't be sure. The microwave beeped at her and she gathered her plate and lantern from the counter. Stopping in the dining room, she grabbed the radio and headed back to her spot on the couch. She had left the news channel on and turned up the volume to listen for updates.

"—Not moving as fast as it first appeared. This one really seems to be lingering over the county. Emergency responders have sent out an announcement that they are still on standby and ready to move as soon as the alert lifts. Hang tight, folks, we're almost out of it."

Addie turned it down and pushed it away. Lingering? Addie couldn't bear the thought. Then the smallest chuckle sent a chill down her spine. Addie instinctively glanced up in the direction of the noise but darted her eyes away just before the shadow could form those eyes again. She could feel the figure there in the corner. Was this because of her?

"You can't let them in," she whispered.

"Why isn't that movie playing?" Addie shouted and stood up to get the movie going. As she waited for the audio to kick in, she hummed to herself and turned back to her crossword. "Is for two, three letters."

"Please help me."

"'Are' of course. There we go." Addie stared down at the book and went over the letters several times.

"Please."

"Shut up!" Addie shouted, tossing her pen before cupping her mouth with both hands. Biscuit perked up.

"You can hear me!" the shadow cried with relief in her voice. Addie shook her head back and forth, humming to herself. She couldn't have. No, she thought. Rule 2, don't engage with them. If you acknowledge them, you let them in. But she had already let *it* in. Her eyes watered. She stood, grabbed the cinnamon, and hastily dumped it around her as she walked over to the corner. The figure shrunk and shifted back to the dining room. Addie looked back at the corner, where cinnamon formed a mound with swirling dust around it. She had emptied the whole container. Addie sighed and tossed it on the floor.

The lights of her bubble flickered, but in her peripheral she saw that the shadow wasn't moving or doing this. They wavered again, and then a full surge struck the house, taking out the television for a split second before everything flashed back on.

"No, no, no," Addie repeated over and over, rocking herself where she sat. Biscuit scooted himself closer to her and rested his face on her feet. "What do we do now, Biscuit?"

"I can help you," the voice whispered. But as the movie came back on, it drowned out her whispers and Addie collected herself. She couldn't let this get to her. It was just a surge, and she still had lanterns, and the generator downstairs. Three surges, Sam had said. At two, get ready, at three, fill the generator. She would still have to figure out how to power the lights. She would probably have to move her sanc-tuary to the kitchen or dining room. Okay, she thought as the lights settled and she took deep breaths to steady her heart.

"I can do this," she said aloud. "I'm going to finish eating, and watch this movie, and not listen to anything else."

"You can't ignore me forever," the voice said gently, but loud enough to hear over the television.

"I can try," Addie whispered to herself.

She got through the whole movie without another surge, but when Addie started the next movie, the second one fell upon the house, a few seconds longer than the first. Even though she had lanterns scat-tered around her, she felt the shadow move while it had room. When the lights came back on, it wasn't in the corner by the stairs. Addie stood and glanced around at the floor, using her peripheral vision to see the shadow standing in the dimness of the dining room.

"They're just outside now," she said. Of course they were outside. They were always outside. But then Addie heard a loud bang, star-tling Biscuit from his nap. His haunches raised and he growled as the sounds circled the house again.

"It's alright, Biscuit, as long as the house is sealed, they can't get in," she told him, though it was more for her own reassurance at this point.

The third surge sent them into darkness again for several seconds. Addie blinked several times, the dim light of the lanterns making her sight blurry until the lights came back on once more. She rubbed her face and cleared her mind. She had to get to the basement. If the power went out and she didn't have the generator started, she didn't know what would happen.

She grabbed what lanterns she could carry and surrounded herself and Biscuit as they slowly made their way back toward the kitchen to the basement door. The basement lights went on without issue, to Addie's relief. It wasn't well-lit, but there was enough light to get to the generator. When she reached it, she saw two containers of gasoline. They were both full.

"Will this keep us safe?" The whisper felt dangerously close to her ear. Biscuit stared into the darkness, in the direction of the voice, but Addie couldn't see anything.

What was she doing? Rule 1, don't look at them. She had done that. Rule 2, don't engage with them. She sighed, knowing she had done that. Rule 3, stay in the light. She was just barely holding onto what was left of that. Rule 4. She thought of the empty container still lying on the floor in the living room. Rule 5... she wasn't supposed to think of Rule 5. But as she stared at the containers of gasoline, she wondered, what was the point now? She could start up the generator, but how much longer could she go? How much effort did she have left in her? Darkness fell over them in a fourth surge. No, not a surge. Several seconds passed and the light overhead didn't come back on. She stood there with Biscuit for another minute, or several, she couldn't tell anymore, the lanterns their only protection now.

"I'm sorry, Biscuit," she said, resigned. "This is my fault." The dog let out a whine and nudged her leg. Addie carefully set down one lantern and grabbed a container of gasoline. "Come on, boy, let's go back upstairs."

Upstairs, she came into the light of the other remaining lanterns in the living room and looked over her house. She and Sam had made this a home together. She hated that he left her. She resented being left alone. Especially with all the memories that held onto the walls and furniture. She unscrewed the cap on the gasoline, the odor filling the air instantly.

"We picked out this coffee table together when I first moved in," she said, turning to the shadow as she lifted the container and splashed gasoline over it. Biscuit jumped back with a whine.

"We cuddled on this couch. I would fall asleep in his arms," she told the shadow, pouring gasoline on the cushions.

"What are you doing?" the shadow asked with worry in her voice. Now she was worried?

"Don't forget the dining table," Addie said as if she just remembered. "This was a gift from his parents when we got married."

"Stop it!"

And with that, she poured more, spreading it in a circle around the rug, and splashing it into the kitchen. Biscuit yelped, still in the living room, avoiding the gasoline spill. Addie coated everything, retracing her steps and heading up the stairs until the container was just about empty. She shook out the last of its contents over the banister and tossed it to the floor.

"Biscuit, where are the matches?" she asked, as if he knew where they would be. He nudged her as she walked past his spot to the end table, finding a matchbook in the drawer.

"You don't want to do that, they'll get in," the shadow cried.

"You are *already* in," Addie responded, looking the shadow in the eye. Those sad eyes, she thought. Addie wondered how it managed to mimic such sadness. She glanced down at Biscuit, now by her side leaning against her. He gave her the same sad eyes. Oh, she thought. I see now.

"You want to go, buddy?" she asked, but Biscuit just put his head in her hand. She patted him and rubbed his ear before ripping a match out of the book.

"No!" the shadow cried, standing in front of her.

"It's okay," Addie whispered.

"Please," the shadow pleaded.

"It's okay," she repeated, and struck the match.

Launch

Henry couldn't remember a time when he wasn't being monitored. The bracelet had grown with him; it was part of his arm. Was he six, or seven? Maybe younger. He didn't remember if he was scared when his parents took him for the implant. He didn't know if it was quick, or painful, if it was on a Tuesday. Much of that didn't matter anyway. He was twenty-two years old now and the program was over. The implant would be removed, the bracelet would come off. As he drove down the highway to the physician's office, he wondered what his parents thought of him. Was he a failure? Or was it a relief that their child wasn't 'the one?' He hadn't bothered to ask; he didn't want to know the answer.

The hero had been named just a few short months ago, someone he didn't know, and now his face was plastered on every billboard and screen in the city. The saviour and protector who would rise up against the invasion and save what was left of mankind. Zavier Martin, scientifically the perfect leader of the American Planetary Guard. He was only nineteen.

It couldn't just be a coincidence that it was announced on the twenty-fifth anniversary of the First Invasion. Henry suspected they had found him long before it was publicly announced since they had called for conscription at the beginning of the year. Frequent attacks is what they cited as the reason for it. Once a year for the past four; Earth was losing the war. The so-called terra-weapons were destroying the land, the southern hemisphere was practically gone. And now after over two hundred years of the draft being a simple formality and back-up plan, it was front and center.

The exit to Meadow Drive had several signs, though the largest and newest was the billboard promoting the APG. Henry tried to ignore it; he already had his conscription notice sitting on his desk at home and the idea of spacewalking wasn't overly appealing. As Henry turned off the busy street into the parking lot, he caught another glimpse of a screen with a loop video of Zavier. He did look positively heroic, the low angle of the camera making him tall and strong against the waving flag as he looked off at some light that made his eyes glisten. His hair was elegantly brushed back, like that old comic book character Henry had read about in school once. Iconic, that was the word. He looked truly iconic.

He wasn't the only one chosen for the APG force; they had a second and third, another man of Henry's age with sleek blonde hair and a menacing brow and a young woman with long dark hair and piercing eyes. They were shown sometimes too, either standing behind Zavier or in smaller pictures under his. Together, they were the heroes of America. The first ones he had ever known in his lifetime, though many names passed through his history books. Together, they would raise the strongest space fleet the world had ever seen. China, Russia, even Britain, wouldn't compare.

The waiting room was cold and sparse; only two others were spread around the room in the chairs lining the walls. The television showed a documentary on the Planetary Guard, featuring Zavier Martin and his crew reviewing blueprints of new vessels and testing new weapons while a voiceover explained the new and improved war efforts and the contributions of the great heroes. The last simulations of their masterful weapon were successful; they were ready for the coming battle. It was only a matter of time until the next invasion, and Zavier and the great Planetary Guard would be waiting for it, ready to defend.

Henry tried not to watch, but he couldn't help listening. The strides of progress being made were impactful, but it made him uneasy. Even with all the preparations, the growing enlistment, and the newfound hope, he was troubled. It didn't feel right; it didn't feel quite real. Henry did not feel hopeful.

Whether the implant was painful or not going in, it certainly was coming out. They had no more local anesthetic to give; he was one of the last ones of the month. He should have waited until the first, the nurse mentioned, when the medical stores were restocked. The slice of his skin was quick, but the jostling of the implant was awful. It had moved; they had to slice again. Instruments, then fingers, bumped around beneath his skin until finally they found it, tore through the blood and muscle, and cauterized both cuts.

An hour he had to wait before the nurses would allow him to drive again, but even then they didn't quite trust him to be well enough and gave him concerned glances. They had the implant in a bag at the desk when he checked out. Some liked to keep it, they explained. He pushed it over the counter into the trash and walked out. What did they think he'd do with it, frame it? The new scars on his arm would be enough of a reminder.

Down Meadow Drive again, Henry turned onto Pearl Street, the opposite direction of home, heading to the only place he felt comfortable. He hadn't told his parents he had finally scheduled the appointment and now he dreaded the idea of them seeing his arm. He had been avoiding extended time with them following the announcement. Seeing the scars might prompt them to try talking to him about it, and he wasn't ready for that. So, to push that off as long as he could, he found himself in The Loft, the small bar wedged in the middle of their small downtown. His friend Jon looked up from pouring drinks to nod to him briefly before going back to serving customers.

It was busy for an afternoon, tables all filled, and the bar spotted with people. His spot was reserved, of course, so he eased through the crowd to find his usual black stool. At the bar, he saw all the televisions on the same channel. It was launch day. How could he have forgotten? When he woke up this morning, he hadn't even thought about it. Now it made sense why the doctor's office had availability today. He wouldn't have minded if his procedure made him miss the whole thing, he really couldn't stand all the hype around it, but he was sure everyone would be on breaks to tune in.

The cameras panned over the crew, headed by Zavier, who were all suited up and walking out to the platform, waving to their audience. The crowd at the site was elated, waving signs of celebration and well wishes, some groups jumping up and down. The bar grew louder with excitement. Jon placed a drink in front of Henry, took a long look at the new wounds on his arm, and grimaced before revealing his own botched X scar. He poured more drinks and glanced at the television in between passing them out. It was a thrilling sight, the heroes finally ascending. Henry could feel the rush of emotions from everyone around him. It was amazing, he couldn't deny it. But somehow he didn't feel connected to it all. It wasn't envy, he decided. He really didn't want to be a hero or a fighter; he just wanted to have his life. Maybe that's what it was, he wondered. Zavier, the others, all of these people around him, they were committed. They wanted to fight for their freedom and believed they could. Henry wasn't a coward, but he felt a sense of guilt for not wanting to join the fight.

Zavier dove into a speech about fighting for humanity, protecting civilization at all costs, and the great lengths he and the heroes had gone to for this moment. He thanked the government for the monitoring program, and his parents for raising him to be strong, all the great things a hero should say. It made Henry roll his eyes, but around him, he felt the ladies swoon and some men nod in solidarity. The other heroes spoke too, just a few words and mostly about the next steps, no 'from-the-heart' speech like Zavier's.

The group then turned away from the cameras and ascended the elevator up to the ship, waving at the top before ducking inside. A few fixed cameras inside showed them being strapped down and checking over the protocols, while the cameras outside showed the rockets beneath them heating up, the air wrinkling and dust scattering, and the cameras inside the launch room daring close-ups of the managers, clearing them for launch. Henry wondered how soon the cameras would be set up at the space station, showing how the heroes glide in zero gravity and finish up the logistics of their weapon, The Grandeur. After months of tests on Earth, they were finally going to put it to use. They didn't ever show the full weapon, only some schematics or parts they had worked on. It was too critical to risk the plans getting into the hands of the enemy. No one really knew how much of Earth's communications were penetrable.

The launch room was anxious, everyone fixed to their computers, focused on the task at hand. The commander communicated inaudibly to the ship and motioned back to the room multiple times. He was a conductor orchestrating the most important piece of their lives, Henry thought. It was methodical and precise, putting everything into place. The camera zoomed into the commander's face as he walked through every detail, his expression so stern Henry could feel the tension.

The countdown began. The bar grew silent, drawing their breath in excitement. 4...3...2...1... the flash of the engines and the tremble of the cameras shook some of the viewers next to Henry, but their eyes were all fixated. The crew was giggling, the force of lift-off slamming them in their seats was real this time, no longer a simulation. The whirl of white and yellow beaming below the rocket leapt out toward the camera as they ascended, leaving a trail of smoke in its wake. The launch room was quiet, following the climb and controls as the heroes headed for the station. Henry found himself holding his breath and could feel his heart beating.

Then the flash of the engines soared upward, blazing white and orange and red, enveloping the ship. White filled the screen and the camera zoomed out as the trail slowed and curved, spurting out smaller tendrils of smoke like a firework. The trail ended. Henry stared at the television, realizing the ship was gone. It took the rest of the bar some time to realize as the smoke came into focus, the stillness turned into gasps and cries and looking around for answers. Chills swept over Henry as he continued watching wide-eyed as panic rose in the launch room, the commander pointing and giving orders before the cameras were cut off, leaving only the outside. The only scene they had left to stare at was the smoke trail and the descent of the rocket's pieces. The reporter was trying to describe what happened and the feeling at the site while remaining composed, but it was all obvious. Everyone at the bar felt it too. The ship was gone; the heroes were gone. Zavier Martin, the saviour of Earth, and his Grandeur weapon to protect against the coming invasion. Dead. In a matter of seconds.

Henry glimpsed the faces of the crowd around him; they were upset, confused, unsure. Jon met his eyes, a resigned look on his face told Henry he was thinking the same thing at that moment. The heroes were lost; the implants were done; thousands of enlisted soldiers were waiting in several stations orbiting Earth without a commander, with more conscripted on the way. Henry could already sense the last bit of hope being stripped away from the world.

Delivery Day

Delivery day. Kate knew the feeling the moment she opened her eyes. Fumbling around the nightstand, her hand met her phone and her eyes found the notification on the screen. She had been waiting all week for her deliveries. She breathed a sigh of relief, thinking how she was running out of her favourite hazelnut coffee. She would have hated to have to actually go to a supermarket to buy some. She loathed the mandated delivery day and wondered if there would ever come a day when they would lift the restriction. But nothing was likely to ever go back to the way it was.

Hers was set for between 10:00 and 11:00. Perfect. It was just enough time for her to shower and head downstairs for breakfast to wait impatiently for all her subscribed goods and new purchases to arrive. Once she was ready, hair combed and fresh loungewear on for working from home, she transcended the stairs and made her way to the kitchen to see what was on her meal plan for the day. Eggs on toast, a green superfood smoothie, and an empty coffee mug that would have to wait to be filled. And then 10:33 the notification popped up on her phone that the delivery truck was six stops away.

By the time she gulped down her smoothie, Kate was ready. The excitement was building; every Thursday became a holiday of unboxing new arrivals for her. The video of her front door popped up on her interactive display as the delivery driver set off the motion sensor and she rose from the dining table. It was strange, she thought, he didn't seem to be carrying anything except a tablet. She watched him on the camera as he rang the doorbell and waited for her and she hesitantly approached the door.

"Good morning," she said, standing with the screen door between them, still looking curiously for her packages. He didn't even bother to look up.

"I just need you to sign for the delivery and I'll drop it off," he said in a rather mundane tone. She didn't remember having any packages that required a signature for this week. But she must have forgotten about something; another wine order maybe? He didn't ask for ID.

"Sure," she said finally, opening the screen door and stepping out to wave her finger across the tablet.

"Alright, I'll be right up," he said with a few taps on the tablet.

"Great, you can just leave it all right here," she said, leaving the screen open. She walked back to the kitchen to clear off the dining table for her boxes. She liked unpacking all the boxes on the table and laying everything out to sort. With the dishes in the sink and the flower centerpiece on the sideboard, she went back to the front door, seeing the delivery van pulling away down the street through the open window.

But she stopped in the foyer, staring at the open doorway that was devoid of brown packaging. Instead, a young boy was standing on her welcome mat with a blank and unsure face.

"Can I help you?" she asked, looking past him at the delivery van shrinking from sight down the street. There was nothing else around, but she had to wonder if he was a pawn in a theft plot, perhaps a distraction while his friends made off with all her boxes.

As if realizing she was there, he pulled a card out of his shirt pocket and put on a sheepish smile. He had to be maybe 5 or 6, but dressed like a little old man, with a vest and argyle socks to go.

"What, are you a gram or something?" she asked. "Where are my packages?"

She walked over and took the card while the boy continued to stare at her with big blue eyes and that awkward grin. The front of the card read Welcome to the beta Amethyst Parenting Program and Kate blinked a few times, wondering if that was correct. She opened the card:

Thank you for becoming parents to the world's best children. Your child was raised in a world-class facility, educated in arts and sciences, trained in specialized skills, and nurtured just for you. This child was hand-selected for you based on your traits; you are a perfect match. As you introduce your beta Amethyst child to the world, remember a few things—

Kate looked back up at the child, who just stood there awkwardly. There had to be some mistake, she thought. A beta parenting program? The idea might have been insane a few years ago, but ever since the pandemic and the population decline and all, she could only roll her eyes at it now. But not for her, certainly. Who would give her a kid? She looked at the card again, then back to the kid.

"Um, hold on," she said. She went into her phone and pulled up her deliveries. Sure enough, everything still showed as pending. She clicked on the chat line and quickly brought up customer support.

"Thank you for reaching out to Customer Support. My name is Brandon, how can I assist you today?"

"Hi, you delivered a child to my door?"

"Yes, we are now partnering with Amethyst Parenting Solutions to provide safe delivery of your child. Did you run into any issues with us getting your child to you?"

"Well, the issue is it isn't my child."

"Oh, that does seem to be an issue. Do you know what child was supposed to be coming?"

"None, that's the point."

"Uh-huh, well, ma'am, I am looking at the address attached to the phone number you're calling from and I do see an Amethyst delivery. I do see that you signed for it and accepted the child. So at this point, there is nothing more I can do on my end since the delivery is complete. Is there anything else I can help you with?"

Kate didn't bother to finish the conversation, hanging up and doing everything she could not to toss her phone on the floor. She took a long deep breath from her nose and looked back at the thing on her doorstep.

"So what are you supposed to do?" she asked. The boy shrugged, then widened his eyes and straightened up as if remembering something.

"Based on the profile you gave me, I am an artistic. I am well-versed in a variety of art media, such as acrylics and watercolour, and I practice piano," he recited. The profile? This was too weird, she thought.

She ushered the boy inside and shut the door. She couldn't very well leave the poor child standing on the porch after all. He immediately took that as an invitation to relax, dropping his shoulders and kicking off his shoes that looked brand new and uncomfortable. He then proceeded to the living room to sit on the sofa and stare at Kate, waiting for instruction. Kate walked over to him and crouched in front of him to meet his eyes.

"What's your name?"

"I don't have one. You're supposed to give me a name," he told her, tapping on the card he gave her. She probably should have finished reading.

"Okay, let's see. 'Remember a few things: Amethyst children are inherently perfect, fully immunized, and free of genetic anomalies. They are ready to explore their new surroundings, but they have not been exposed to meat-based diets, extreme temperatures, or pets. Amethyst children do not have given names to provide a bonding experience with you as their new parent. Your Nurture credit will be in your account prior to delivery. Please contact Customer Service with questions.'

Contact Customer Service? Perfect. I just have to call and tell them this is a mistake," Kate said.

"A mistake?"

Kate eyed the confused boy. "Yeah, I'm not your mom. I didn't sign up for this. You're supposed to go somewhere else."

The boy seemed to think on that for a minute, then shrugged again and leaned back in the sofa, waiting for the next instruction. He started swinging his legs up and down while Kate took out her phone to dial the Customer Service number. After punching through all the prompts, the line finally started ringing.

"Thank you for calling Amethyst Parenting Solutions, providing the world's best children. My name is Soleil, what can I help you with?" the cheery voice on the other end said.

"Hi, yeah, I just received a child today," Kate began.

"Oh congratulations," Soleil interrupted.

"Uh, no. No, I never ordered or requested, I never signed up for this. It isn't my kid," she explained. She realized she didn't even know the proper term for it. If it was delivered, was it an order? How did you even go about getting a kid this way, she wondered.

"Oh my, let's look into this," Soleil said, changing her tone from overtly cheery to shocked but somehow still upbeat. She also wondered how some customer support people managed that.

"Okay, what is the address?" she asked, and Kate gave her address. "Okay, yes I do see a child was delivered to that address and signed for."

"Yes, he's sitting in my living room."

"Yes, so what we can do now is fill out a mis-delivery complaint and get that to the problem-solving team so they can match the child's designation with the family in our system."

"And what happens in the meantime?"

"Well if I can get your contact information, we'll reach out if we have any further questions."

"That's it?"

"Well, yes."

"How long is that supposed to take?"

"I'm not sure. The problem-solving team's turnaround time is 24-48 hours."

"And what am I supposed to do with the kid?"

"Oh," she said, as if realizing the gravity of the situation. "Let me just put this into the escalation pile. Or you know, I'll just take it right to my manager. And I'll get back to you as soon as I have an answer for you."

When they got off the phone, Kate sighed, wondering how this could happen. Why would they deliver children without an escort, and why wouldn't they be taking this more seriously? What if he was mistakenly delivered to a serial killer or pedophile? Kate thought. This was crazy. And how were these parents vetted anyway, what were these people like that they could just buy a child online? Kate went over to the loveseat across from the boy and sat down with another heavy sigh, sinking into the grey cushions. The boy stopped kicking his legs and sat up straight, waiting for her.

"Have you thought of my name yet?" he asked nicely, with his hands on his lap. She could tell he was straining to keep still now that she was in front of him.

"What do you want your name to be?" she asked. He scrunched his eyebrows, and she wondered if he was confused by the question or the fact that he was being asked for his own opinion. But then he smirked.

"Toby!" he said with excitement.

"Toby? From that cartoon?"

"Bran and Friends," he told her. "He's my favourite character."

"Toby it is," Kate said. She couldn't help but smile at his happiness.

"I'm hungry," he said, twisting his face as his stomach growled. Realizing she didn't really have much food in the house since her actual packages weren't delivered, she thought about what they could eat. It was still early, but some places would be opening for lunch now. She remembered the card said these kids were vegetarians.

"What kind of food do you eat?"

Toby sat up and cleared his throat as if preparing a speech. "We are raised on a plant-based diet of vegetables, fruits, nuts, beans, and whole grains. We were often exposed to different cuisines to expand our flavour palette." He looked up for a second and then nodded and smiled at Kate.

"Do you like those foods?" she asked.

"Some of them," he said hesitantly, thinking about it. "I like noodles."

She smirked at that and quickly sent an email to her boss explaining that she'd need time today to sort out a "personal matter." How else was she going to explain this? It sounded unreal even to her, and the kid was right in front of her.

With that, they were in the car on their way to the little pasta place down the street. He didn't speak the entire time in the car. When she checked on him in the rearview, she saw him staring out the window with wide eyes, as if he had never been in a town before. He seemed so small for the seat; he probably should have been in a car seat at that age. They arrived at the restaurant, where the waitress gave Toby a big smile and led them to a booth enclosed in plexiglass on both sides.

"So what do you want to eat?" Kate asked Toby as he scanned the menu with his little fingers.

"This one!" he said, loosening that stiff automated façade a little more. Kate inspected the menu and saw he was pointing at spaghetti and meatballs.

"You're not supposed to eat meat," Kate said.

Toby scrunched his face. "Well, you're my mom now, you decide what I can eat."

"I'm not your mom, remember? And maybe your real mom will want you to be vegetarian still."

Toby's eyes dropped and he pouted his lip. Kate rolled her eyes; he was a pretty cute kid.

"But I won't tell her if you won't," Kate reasoned, and Toby lit up again, probably at the idea of having a secret on top of eating meatballs.

The spaghetti came out steaming and Toby licked his lips at the hill of pasta and meatballs.

"Do you want cheese?" the waitress asked and Toby nodded fervently, watching the shaved cheese build on top. Kate waved a hand after seeing the cheese multiply without Toby telling her 'when' and took a more conservative serving of cheese on her own spaghetti. Toby dove in with his fork and ate proudly.

"Careful," Kate said. "You eat too fast and you'll get a tummy ache."

"I love noodles! I always eat more noodles than the other boys," Toby said with orange lips.

Kate unfolded his napkin and gave it to him. "Were there a lot of children with you?"

Toby nodded as he wiped at his mouth. "All Amethyst children spend their first years in a co—co..." he started, but got stuck on a word. "Co-wort."

"Cohort," Kate pronounced. Toby scrunched his nose and continued without repeating it.

"We sleep in group quarters and spend time learning socialization. We attend elementary classes together and," he paused again, thinking. "And receive individual instruction based on our profile."

"Did you like it?"

"I liked maths, but they told me I had to learn piano. But then after we got to play in the park together, and that was fun."

Kate thought about the process, imagined the type of facility they were raised in. Was there no nurture? It seemed they were just bred to learn and be good. But it was a beta program, she remembered. Maybe the parents didn't know what they were actually signing up for, or how the program worked behind the scenes.

Toby practically slurped up his entire meal, making an orange ring of sauce around his face. The waitress brought over wet wipes and Toby patiently let Kate clean his face. When they were done and paid, he hopped down from his seat and grabbed Kate's hand. Kate looked down at their hands together and gingerly accepted it before they walked out to the car. On the ride home, Kate let the windows down and Toby sat forward to feel the wind mess his hair.

"Oh! Look!" he shouted through the wind, pointing out the window as they came to the light. Kate saw he was pointing to a park where one other kid was swinging. "Can we go?"

Kate hesitated. "We really should be home in case they figure out how to get you to your parents."

"But that could take forever," he moaned and leaned back in the seat dramatically. Kate laughed and rolled her eyes as the light turned green and found herself turning into the parking lot.

"Alright, you can have 15 minutes," she said as he perked up. She let him out of the car and handed him a mask. "But you need to wear this."

"Why?" he asked, taking it.

"Because other people might be sick. You see the girl is wearing one too, and her mom."

"But I don't get sick, Misses M told us so," he said, muffled through the mask.

"Yep, well, that family over there doesn't know that."

Toby shrugged but didn't fuss. He skipped along to the swings and waved to the girl on the other end. He started with sitting properly and got as high as he could. Then he jumped off and looked back at Kate with a sly look in his eye. Kate watched as he turned back to the swing and jumped onto it belly first and started spinning around. And Kate rubbed his back as he threw up some of his spaghetti by the car before they headed home.

"How are you feeling?" she asked him as she handed him a glass of water and they settled on the couch at home.

"I feel better now," he said and took a big gulp of water.

"Good, how about a movie now? We'll leave playing for later," she said and he nodded. She let him pick the movie, one of the newest animated musicals. She checked her phone but didn't have any notifications. As the music played, Toby danced along.

"Something else now!" Toby said as the credits rolled.

"Alright, well," she said, thinking. "Do you want to show me your art skills? You learned drawing, right?"

Toby scrunched his nose. "Yeah, I guess."

She took out paper and coloured pencils and set him up on the dining table. Together, they drew different pictures. She drew some flowers slowly, watching him as he drew a realistic plate of spaghetti and meatballs, then a rough sketch of the park exactly as it was laid out, and finally a near-perfect imitation of the protagonist from the movie they watched.

"Wow, that's really good. You drew all this from memory?" she said as he dropped his pencil and handed her the paper.

"Mr. C said it's eye—eye..."

"Eidetic," she pronounced for him. He nodded again without repeating it.

"I usually work with paints and like to apply impressionist methods," he recited with a smirk.

He helped her clean up and they happily moved on to the next thing. The afternoon flew by and they played a few board games, though Toby, having never played them before, made up his own rules and stuck out his tongue when Kate called him a cheater. He refused to nap and insisted on snacks every other hour, cleaning out the rest of Kate's pantry. She ordered a pizza for dinner, checking her phone again to see nothing. No update from Amethyst.

"I'm going to eat the whole pizza by myself!" Toby shouted eagerly when the doorbell rang. They were not allowed pizza, he had explained, but Bran and friends ate pizza all the time, so it must be good. Kate shook her head and chuckled before opening the door. But in front of her were two police officers.

"Oh, hello," she said, putting her purse and cash down.

"Kathryn Williams?" the older man asked through the screen.

"Yes?" she replied nervously.

"Hello ma'am, I'm Officer Swanson, this is my partner Officer Bernard. May we come in and ask you a few questions?" Kate cautiously opened the screen and stepped back to maintain appropriate distance.

"What is this about?" she asked as they stood stiffly by the door.

"We had a family in this neighbourhood report a missing child, and received information that you were seen with a child earlier today."

Kate blinked a few times, realizing they meant Toby. "Oh, um, yes, he was delivered today. I've been waiting for someone to get back to me."

The officers quickly exchanged exasperated looks.

"I'm sorry, did you say 'delivered'?" the older man asked and paused. "As in, Amethyst Solutions?"

"I told them he wasn't mine," she explained and remembered she had the card in her back pocket. She pulled it out and showed them. "They said they were looking into it. I didn't have anywhere to bring him, so he's just been here. Did you find his parents?"

Swanson sighed while shaking his head and Bernard shut his notebook and tucked it away in his pocket.

"Yes, ma'am, we're working with the family to retrieve the child."

"He's in the living room watching TV. Sir, I promise, this—I didn't—," she tried.

Officer Bernard nodded. "It's alright, ma'am. Unfortunately, this is not the first instance of a—mis-delivered Amethyst child. It's the third one in our precinct alone."

"If we can just bring him to his home now, we'd appreciate your cooperation," Officer Swanson added. She led them into the living room, where Toby stood up on the couch upon seeing them enter.

"Pizza!" he said.

Kate smiled at him. "No, buddy. These are police officers. You know what that is, right?"

Toby nodded and hopped off the couch.

"They figured out who your mom and dad are, so they can take you home now," she told him.

"But I don't wanna, I want pizza!" he said and sunk into the couch.

"Well, your parents might have pizza or some other dinner waiting for you. They've been really worried about you," she said, sitting on the couch next to him and grabbing his shoes.

The younger officer knelt beside them. "Hey, bud. We're going to get you to your parents, yeah? Did you have fun today with Kathryn?"

"Oh yeah, she's awesome. We watched movies and I won all the games and I got to eat meatballs!"

Kate glanced at the officer with a guilty face and the officer smirked at her. She got Toby's shoes tied and scooted him off the couch. She walked them to the front door but didn't want to follow them out. Toby looked back at her and stopped.

"Aren't you coming?" he asked.

"No, I stay here. You'll be okay with them," she said.

"Will I see you again?" he asked.

"I think you live nearby so probably, I'll see you around," she said, not sure if that would be true.

He looked down at his feet and then back at her with sad puppy eyes.

"But what if I don't like them?"

Kate looked at the officers and then crouched down to face Toby. "I bet you're going to love them, and they're going to love you. And you'll have a lot of fun."

Toby wrapped his arms around Kate's neck and she hugged him back, patted him on the head, and stood up. The older officer took him by the hand and walked him down to the car, but the younger man lingered.

"I'm sorry for the misunderstanding. We're looking into this whole thing with Amethyst," he said, trying to reassure her.

"Thank you. I mean, just dropping children on doorsteps?" she said with raised eyebrows as she leaned in the doorway.

"Again, we appreciate you cooperating with us and handing him over," he said.

"Of course, of course. I don't even want kids, so all the better," she said with a laugh.

The officer nodded. "Have a good night."

She closed the screen and waited for the car to leave, watching the lights head down the street and disappear around the turn. She shut the door and walked back to the living room. It was a strange day, having to deal with that curve ball. The TV was still playing some kids' show Toby was watching. She turned it off and then looked around. It was quiet. She sat down with a sigh, then pulled out her phone and opened the shopping app. Her delivery was still pending after all that. It was time to contact customer service again.

Station 217

"Attention, everyone," the captain raised his voice as he entered the work forum. The room was dim, but that's how they seemed to like it. The light from their screens made their faces glow as they stopped what they were doing and eyed him over the equipment. His group of twenty subordinates looked concerned already; it was rare he addressed the whole room.

"Thank you. I want to inform you that the Chancellor is visiting; he should be here any moment. I want you all to continue working like normal. This is a standard inspection of work, so he wants to see you working. If anyone has any questions, please let me know now," the captain said over the room.

"What is he inspecting?" Cassandra asked. Of course Cassandra was the one to ask for all of them.

"He's just here to see how we are all getting on, to see how effective the program is. He may ask you questions, but don't be nervous. There is nothing to worry about."

"I think you have something to worry about," Alex said from his station to Carol behind him.

"What are you talking about?" Carol asked him, waving her hands at her screens.

"You are failing. Look at all your assignments; you can't even keep them organized. War, famine, it's horrible."

"They are all doing just fine and quite to plan, thank you very much," she said.

"If you say so," Alex chided.

"Everyone, please welcome the Chancellor to Station 217," the captain addressed the room once more.

"Hello," they said. "Pleasure."

"How wonderful it is to be here with you all," the Chancellor greeted, cupping his hands and giving a slight bow to the room. "I look forward to seeing all of your assignments and the exceptional progress that has been going on in this sector."

"It is a pleasure to have you, Chancellor," the captain said. "Please let me know if you need anything; otherwise, I will leave you to it."

"Thank you, Captain. I think I'll just take a look around for now. I'm seeing quite a lot going on your screens." And with that, the Chancellor embarked on a rather slow trek weaving through workstations with the captain trailing close behind, nervously fiddling with his hands behind his back.

"Excuse me miss, what is your name?" the Chancellor asked as he finally paused at one station.

"Cassandra," the woman said nervously. She moved aside to let him in as he neared her desk while the captain looked on.

"Tell me Cassandra, what are you working on?"

"Well, I just started here not long ago. I'm up to my third assignment. My first is right here. As you can see, it's been very successful. Things are moving just as I expected as per the timeline. They are getting ready for a huge advancement, a giant step in flight technology. My second one right here, this one was off to a rocky start. We had an inexplicable natural disaster that nearly wiped out the entire civilization. But now that it's up and running again, they *are* moving along per the timeline. They have just introduced religion and a hierarchy in society. We should be looking forward to roads and the first empire in about twenty rotations."

"I see, wonderful, wonderful. Now where is your third assignment?"

"That is right here. We merely just begun here as you can see. There are still numerous human populations roaming separately but I developed a timeline for them all to come together and they should start forming civilization after I introduce some external motivation."

"What kind of 'external motivation' are you thinking of?"

"I was going to start with altering migration patterns for the animals and then possibly introduce some natural disasters that change the landscape so the human populations will migrate toward each other in a more sustainable area for growth."

"Fabulous. It looks like you caught on quickly in this. Thank you very much for showing me that."

"Thank you, sir. It's been an honour to work here." Cassandra bared a smile and looked at the captain, who gave a reassuring nod.

"Now who do we have next; what's your name?"

"Alex, sir."

"Well Alex, it looks like you have a very extensive portfolio."

"Indeed," the captain chimed in. "Alex is our most senior team member here." Alex smirked and tilted his head with a modest shrug.

"Well, tell me about your current projects."

"I successfully jump started around fifteen assignments now in my five rotations here. Four of them are so far advanced they've surpassed my control and have developed their own way through the universe. Three of them are at the peak of developing space technology; they should be venturing out of their solar systems soon. Another four are in the early developmental stages, two of them I have just begun and haven't developed a full-scale plan for them yet."

Alex spun in his chair and pulled up several windows of his screen before turning back to the Chancellor. "These two, I think you'll find interesting, sir. This one, I call A Kappa 16, is right at the brink of artificial intelligence taking over."

"Hm. Fascinating; how did you plan for that?" the Chancellor asked, taking a closer look at the data.

"Well, to be honest, I didn't. The idea came to me when I saw them developing robotics and their fascination with superiority. They are so strong-minded at the top of the food chain that their only worry is having their knowledge surpassed. So I thought I would make their fears a reality and I gave the artificial intelligence a little boost on my own."

"Now, we don't normally encourage interference this way, but I think you're onto a solid idea. I'd like to keep posted on the progress of that one."

"Absolutely, sir," Alex said assuredly. Behind the Chancellor, the captain rolled his eyes at Alex's confidence, but he was his best associate, so he let him continue. "This second one I want to show you recently had a pandemic that wiped out half the population. I didn't intend for it to be so big, but once it started, I thought I would let it roll organically and see where it went. They have since abandoned technology and reverted to a sort of Stone Age, forming smaller societies and avoiding masses again to prevent the disease from spreading."

"Interesting, and how does that help us?"

"Well, sir, it's giving me time to observe and understand how certain human populations react in adversity. You see, one of my other assignments over here had the same type of pandemic not too long ago. I was having an issue with overpopulation and not hitting my target for space technology advancement, and so introduced this as a way to give me more time. Indeed, the idea of losing half the population made them advance even further by way of biotechnology advancements. They now have artificial procreation and genetically engineered humans who evolve more quickly to their surroundings."

"So you're saying the same factors don't always give the same outcome," the Chancellor concluded and Alex nodded.

"I'm keeping an eye on this one to see how several smaller societies develop versus one larger one. I think with the siloed groups, we may get more variety in how they choose to advance."

"Fascinating, bringing in a little anthropology. It sounds like your assignments have been very successful."

"Quite so, sir, I have learned much in my time and feel I've contributed incredible insight to this institution." The captain held in a laugh; it seemed the Chancellor was taken with Alex's charisma and didn't see the pandering.

"Very well, we are glad to have you on board. Now let's see, who are you?" the Chancellor said, moving onto another workstation.

"My name is Carol."

"Well, Carol, it looks like you have a few off to a good start. Why don't you tell me what you are working on?"

"Well, I have six assignments currently in progress. One of them has been extremely successful and advanced quite quickly. They are about five rotations ahead of my planned timeline, which has never happened before. They are working through the early development of space technology and robotics.

"Very nice, I like seeing the different developmental stages from everyone. Now, what is that one?" he pointed to one screen of data where the captain immediately saw flaws and marks on the timeline.

"Oh, that's one the citizens call Earth. I call them by their formed names, you see. That one is a rather troublesome assignment."

"Troublesome, eh? How so?"

"Well, how do I describe it? They can't seem to get war out of their minds."

"War?"

"Yes, sir. It is very difficult to force advancements on them when they keep reverting back to basic warfare. Now, don't get me wrong; some of this warfare has led to advancements in communication and societal changes. It was the only way to get nuclear technology on time. And for a time they were focusing on space technology, which should have led to the start of global socialism. But instead, the nations continue to develop separately and compete in these advancements, which prevents the best technology from moving forward."

"Interesting. Wow, that puts your planet nearly one hundred rotations behind your timeline."

"I know. You see for nearly two thousand rotations, they were perfectly on time, and they slowly started tapering off, making different choices than I was expecting."

"Are they still on religious squabbles? At this point, with this much advancement, they should be tapping into AI and eliminating religion altogether.”

“Exactly, sir. I don't understand how to fix it.”

“Captain, have you been working on any plans to adjust, or is it a lost cause?”

“Yes,” the captain spoke up and stepped closer. “Yes, we've come up with an adjustment to the timeline involving an extraterrestrial invasion to force international cooperation. This should accommodate for a faster advancement through the next hundred rotations.”

“I should like to keep posted about that,” he said with concern. It was rare they ever had to scrap a project for advancement failure, so the captain gave a quick and serious nod before the Chancellor turned back to Carol. “What about your others?”

“Well, they have been going much better than this one.”

“Show me that one; number four.”

“Oh, not number four, you don't want to see that. That one is a bit of an experiment.”

“What do you mean an experiment; they are all experiments?”

“I know, sir, but with the advancements they've been making, there is a point where I wanted to introduce something outrageous.”

“And what have you done that is *outrageous*?” he asked curiously. The captain watched with worry; he had not informed the Chancellor of this yet.

“Well, Alex and I have teamed up and one of his more advanced planets is going to observe this one and attempt to make contact. Lirra, that's what they call their planet, is just starting to get ideas of alien races, I thought it was good timing."

"Well," the Chancellor said, looking back over at Alex, who was still watching and listening. "I can't say that's terribly outrageous. When I was in your position many rotations ago I did a very similar thing; they were very early on in their civilization, still forming ideas and learning how to convey them. The alien visitors created a religion so deep within the race that I failed to eliminate it when the time came for their further advancement. To this rotation, they still believe in a group of gods they call the Sacred Nine." The captain felt a wave of relief, and in the corner of his eye, he could see Alex punch the air in celebration.

"Incredible, sir, I didn't know you were a Creator before this. I can't say the same thing will happen in this situation; they are further advanced in approaching atheism. But I think it will jumpstart the desire to travel and learn more about their galaxy. At least that's what I'm hoping for."

"Yes, well you keep it up. Now, what's going on with number six, why does that look peculiar?"

"That one was invaded not long ago."

"On purpose?"

"No, it was actually out of our control. When we founded this planet, Plo, we did not realize the neighboring solar system was home to a warrior race. Once Plo was advanced enough, it basically sent a beacon out to space. The warriors are some shadow race that we hadn't detected. They descended upon them within a few rotations and have been slowly assimilating all the humans. We can no longer manipulate what's left and the planet will be gone within the next ten rotations."

"Well, that is disappointing. We put so much effort into growing these planets from scratch. We need to take more precautions in where we place them."

"Certainly, sir," the captain answered. "We have since updated all of our scanners to include the technology and energy fields that this species was using and have avoided several divisions in this sector following that unfortunate circumstance."

"Good to hear, good to hear."

Carol smiled gingerly. "I am putting a plan together for my next planet. I will submit a proposal tomorrow and we will see how it turns out."

"Good luck with your next proposition."

"Thank you, sir."

"Well, Captain. It seems that most of these projects are going rather well and shaping up to be very solid experiments. If they are half as successful as mine were, I think this team will be solid."

"Oh my," Alex said.

"What is it?" Carol asked as the captain eyed him. The Chancellor was nearly done.

"No no no," Alex said.

"Alex, what's going on?" the captain snapped, and the Chancellor's attention moved to Alex's screens.

"They've discovered us," was all he said and stopped both the captain and Chancellor in their steps.

"Who has?" Cassandra chimed in.

"MC Delta 6, my most advanced planet." Alex stared frozen at his screen in disbelief.

"What do you mean?" Carol asked.

"What is going on, what is the meaning of this?" the Chancellor commanded, looking to the captain for an answer.

"I don't know, it's something I missed. It seems that technology was so advanced, that they were looking for something more, other planets and other spaceships, but I didn't think we would come under their radar. We're so far away."

"We shouldn't have," the captain said, eyeing the screen. "We are far more advanced than any of these should be. They don't learn about us unless we want them to."

Alex turned to them, his face still in awe. "Well, it seems they just launched a ship toward us and they're going to make contact."

The Chancellor shook his head. "Shoot them down."

"But Chancellor we can't do that," the captain said. "Can we?"

"Yes, we can. This is now a failed experiment, and I am ending it."

"I put so much time into MC Delta 6; they are coming to see their Creator!" Alex whined.

"You are not God!" the Chancellor bellowed.

"But would this not be the next step in our experiments? The ultimate test; what will they do when they learn their whole existence is a lie!" Alex yelled in a newfound excitement.

The Captain pushed him away. "Alex, you are relieved of your post effective immediately. This is out of hand."

"Sir, please don't hurt them. Give me another chance; let me do this."

"Captain, end this now. Enable Protocol 88. We cannot be discovered," The Chancellor said angrily but clearly hiding a worry the captain shared.

"Protocol 88? Chancellor," the captain started, unsure. They'd never had to do that before.

"Captain, I just received a signal. Someone is trying to hail us," Cassandra said, reading the screen. Several others voiced the same notification, and slowly, the same thing appeared on every single screen.

"Answer them!" Alex shouted.

"Do not!" the Chancellor boomed. "Captain, control your team or I will relieve *you* of duty."

"Hello? Is it on? *I don't think it's on. Oh, it is, oh boy.* Hello?" a voice sounded through the room. The room fell silent. "Okay, hello! Greetings. We have travelled far and at last, come to you in peace. If you can understand us, please answer."

The room remained silent. The captain looked at Alex, who was now stunned into silence at the sound of his people, and then to the Chancellor, who seemed scared now.

"*I don't know. Maybe they can't,*" the voice said again, not directed at the station. "Hello?"

The room was still and uncertain.

"What do we do, Chancellor?"